Liquid Gold
The Lore and Logic of Using Urine to Grow Plants

Carol Steinfeld

ecowaters books

USA

Ecowaters Books is a project of Ecowaters Projects

www.ecowaters.org

ECOWATERS PROJECTS

Printed on acid-free recycled-content paper with soy-based inks

Washwater Garden™ and GROW (Garden Recycling of Wastewater) System™
are trademarks of the Ecological Engineering Group

Published by:
Ecowaters Books

For information about permission to reprint excerpts
of this book, write to:
   info@liquidgoldbook.com

   Liquid Gold
   c/o Ecowaters Permissions
   P.O. Box 1330
   Concord, MA 01742-1330

Steinfeld, Carol
Liquid Gold

ISBN: 978-0-9666783-1-4
1. Water. 2. Humor. 3. Garden.

Sales of this book help fund the programs of Ecowaters Projects.

Contents

Science and Technology of Using Liquid Gold

Gold to Green: Profiles of Liquid Gold at Work in Gardens and Farms Worldwide

Acknowledgments

Learning to use wastewater and excreta to fertilize and water plants can be life changing. For to truly understand the life systems that support us, we must look at all its resource flows—its inputs and outputs—and how they cycle.

While updating our first book, *The Composting Toilet System Book*, my co-author David Del Porto and I encountered the work of architect and researcher Uno Winblad and several other researchers who advocated the use of toilets that divert urine. Through their reports, we met George Anna Clark, who works with César Añorve to promote and install waterless urine-diverting toilets outside of Mexico City. The Swedish report, "Urine Separating," took the topic further for us, confirming the feasibility of using urine for fertilizer on a larger scale in industrialized countries. We experimented with using urine in various ways to fertilize plants in our homes and office. We were sold! But explaining this concept to the general public was another matter, and that's the purpose of this book.

For this book, thanks are due Uno Winblad, Jan-Olof Drangert, and many other Swedish urine-use researchers; George Anna Clark of Espacio de Salud and César Añorve; Peter Harper of Center for Appropriate Technology in Wales; illustrators, Malcolm Wells, Daniel Harper, and John Kitses; and supporter Sanjay Jain, as well as the many attendees of my waste composting and composting toilet workshops who related bits of urine lore, some of which appear in this book. Thanks to Joe U. Rinal (his Internet nom de plume) for urinal photos from his Web site, www.urinal.net. Much thanks go to Paul Spinrad, author of *The RE/Search Guide to Bodily Fluids* (Juno Books), the book that led me to the informative book, *Scatalogic Rites of All Nations*, by the late John G. Bourke. As always, big thanks are due to systems thinker extraordinaire David Del Porto, my friend and technical advisor, who introduced me to the realm of wastewater recycling. Life has been a lot more interesting ever since.

Updates and links to further resources can be found at this book's Web site: www.liquidgoldbook.com.

Carol Steinfeld

PEE ON EARTH DAY
June 21

(December 21 in the southern hemisphere)

On Pee On Earth Day, take your urine outside to nourish plants and save water by reducing toilet flushing. Use your liquid assets to grow plants and promote resource stability!

- Dilute your urine and apply to plants
- Pour your urine on a compost pile
- Pour your urine on well-aerated soil and mulch
- Disperse it (don't put lots of it in one spot on the soil)

See www.liquidgoldbook.com for updates

Introduction

Urine Defined

From the *Oxford English Dictionary:*
Urine: (greek: ουρον)
The excrementitious fluid secreted from the blood by the kidneys in man and the higher animals, stored in the bladder, and voided at intervals through the urethra.

From *Van Nostrand's Scientific Encyclopedia:*
Urine is the fluid secreted from the blood by the kidneys, stored in the bladder and discharged by the urethra. In healthy humans, it is amber colored. About 1,250 milliliters (about a third of a gallon or 0.044 cubic feet) of urine are excreted in 24 hours with normal specific gravities of 1.024. Flow ranges from 0.5 to 20 milliliters/minute with extremes of dehydration and hydration. Maximum osmolar concentration is 1,400 compared to plasma osmolarity of 300. In diabetes insipidus, volumes of 4 to 6.6 gallons or 15 to 25 liters per day of dilute urine may be formed. In addition to the substances found in the table in the Science and Technology of Using Liquid Gold chapter, there are trace amounts of purine bases and methelated purines, glucuronates, the pigments of urochrome and urobilin, hippuric acid and amino acids. In pathological states, other substances will appear: proteins (nephrosis); bile pigments and salts; glucose, acetone, acetoacetic acid, and beta-hydrobuttyric acid.

A Golden Opportunity!

Every day, Americans excrete about 90 million gallons of urine. That day's urine contains an estimated seven million pounds of nutrients in the form of nitrogen. By some estimates, that's enough to fertilize up to 31,962 acres of corn for an entire year. And over one year, Americans "piss away" enough nitrogen to fertilize almost 12 million acres of corn—about twice the corn grown in Indiana.*

A Resource in the Wrong Place Pollutes

When we flush urine away, it flows to wastewater treatment plants or to septic systems (among other places). These discharge it to the soil, groundwater, streams, lakes, rivers, or seas—often with much of the nitrogen intact.

In lakes and other surface waters, aquatic plants and algae consume the nitrogen, resulting in a great bloom of growth. When this growth dies and decomposes, it pulls oxygen from the water—which can suffocate fish and other aquatic life. Underground, nitrogen can seep into drinking water, posing a potential health hazard. At the same time, farmers worldwide purchase tons of nitrogen fertilizer, much of it from industrial fertilizer factories that produce it with imported energy.

From Pollutant to Fertilizer

Using urine's nitrogen repairs this broken nutrient cycle by putting it

*Widely ranging variables can affect this figure, including growing methods, corn varieties, climate, soils, and diets and ages of the urine contributors.

to work instead of disposing it. Add the fact that urine is usually sterile in healthy populations, and we have a golden opportunity. For those of us who appreciate a good free thing, urine is truly liquid gold— a product of our bodies that can help our trees, plants, and even food crops thrive, saving fertilizer costs and taking a load off our overwhelmed environment.

Safe to Use

Safe methods for using urine to nourish plants are now well documented, particularly in Sweden, where several research institutions and Stockholm's water authority studied the sociology, bacteriology, and viability of collecting urine and applying it to grain crops. Urine is typically sterile before it leaves the body in healthy individuals, and using your own urine cannot give you a disease that you do not already have.

However, it is important to take the precautions noted in this book. Excreta cannot be applied cavalierly: At different times throughout the world, cholera and other disease epidemics resulted from mismanaged excreta, mostly feces. This was usually due to a concentration of too many people of poor health living in one place. Fertilizing with urine, following established methods that assure that any pathogens are stabilized, is a safe practice.

An Age-Old Practice Enters Modern Bathrooms

Separating urine is not new. Populations in numerous countries either urinated into a container separate from feces or used a urine diverter, a drain cast inside the toilet opening. In England, for example, the Earth Closet was a waterless urine-diverting toilet that competed with the water-flush toilet, Thomas Crapper's invention and the precursor of today's flush toilet.

Today, urine-diverting toilet stools—also called urine-separating and no-mix toilets—are manufactured in Sweden, Germany, Poland, Mexico, Africa, and China.

Reducing Wastewater Treatment Costs

Managing wastewater is getting increasingly more expensive. Many countries, including the United States, Canada, and Europe, are requiring wastewater to be treated to a much higher quality than before, as the effects of too many people and too much wastewater contaminate water. In coastal and other environmentally sensitive areas, federal and municipal authorities are requiring the reduction of the nutrients, or *denitrification*, of wastewater to protect water quality. That adds significant costs to wastewater treatment. Where does most of the nutrient content come from? Human urine.

Factor in the cost of nitrogen fertilizer purchased for farms, landscapers, and plant nurseries, and the opportunity to reduce costs while preventing pollution becomes clearer. An expensive management challenge for the wastewater industry is liquid gold to farmers and other growers.

Closer to Home

On an individual level, many people are relieved (you might say) to learn about the scientific validity of using their own liquid gold in their gardens as free fertilizer. It is empowering to know that our body's excretions can feed the plants that feed our bodies—an easy way to reconnect with the cycle of life. And get something for nearly nothing.

Photo: Sven Ingvar-Nilsson

Rev. Thomas Moule's Earth Closet featured a urine diverter and a hopper that dispensed earth and ashes after every "deposit." It competed with the water-flush toilet, for the mass market in 19th-century England. The water-flush toilet won out, perpetuating the "flush and forget" mentality that is so problematic today.

Liquid Gold begins with bits of urine lore to bring levity to this topic and relax our sometimes overdeveloped aversion to urine, which need not be a toxic substance. There is a long human history of using urine, not just for growing crops, but also in rituals, in medicine, and in industry. We advocate using urine only for fertilizing plants. This book concludes with specific ways to use liquid gold for plants and how people worldwide are using liquid gold.

Using urine for plant fertilizer can help clean our lakes and rivers, save water, reduce the cost of wastewater treatment, return nutrients to farmlands, and end the unnecessary over-production of industrial fertilizers.

Think twice before flushing it away!

Reducing Foreign Energy Dependence with Liquid Gold

Trading petroleum for pee-troleum

Collecting and using liquid gold can reduce the United States' need to import foreign energy. It can do that in two ways: (1) Alleviating the need for fertilizers made with imported natural gas, and (2) growing the ingredients of biofuels, which can replace imported fuels.

According to Iowa State University's agronomy department, natural gas is an ingredient in the production of synthetic urea for nitrogen fertilizer. For that reason, nitrogen fertilizer production costs are closely tied to the price of natural gas. Natural gas derived in the U.S. is nearly depleted, so much is imported from other countries, such as Algeria and the Middle East. Natural gas accounts for more than 85 percent of the total ammonia production cost. When the price of natural gas increased in 2001, the cost of nitrogen fertilizer also increased dramatically.

At the same time, biofuels made of biomass (trees, waste paper, sawdust, even sewage sludge), ethanol, grains, vegetable oils, etc. can be grown by American farmers to replace petroleum-derived fuels.

American farmers are in need of new crops to replace tobacco and other crops that compete with foreign imports. (And some farmers still receive subsidies to *not* grow crops at all!) Using local biofuels can prevent fuel shortages and reduce air pollution too.

Instead of investing billions of dollars to reduce nitrogen in wastewater and manage the pollution it causes, we should instead invest in the systems needed to transport wastewater to deserts and brownfields where it can grow biological alternatives to petroleum in North America. The result: less dependence on foreign fuel and foreign policy compromises, more work for Americans, and better environmental health—which means better human health.

Using our liquid gold to grow fuel is true local sufficiency!

Urine Lore

Urine Use Through History

Urine has been used throughout human history for a variety of purposes, from religious rituals and rites of passage to medicinal, culinary, and industrial purposes. And of course, it's been used to fertilize food crops.

Human urine may be the most commonly used bodily excretion, perhaps because it usually does not carry the disease risk that other excretions can. It is almost always sterile before it leaves the body. Swedish anthropologist Jan-Olof Drangert suggests that the taboo against contact with excreta common to many cultures is less pronounced for urine, perhaps because it most closely resembles water.

Attitudes toward urine vary among cultures. Western and Middle Eastern cultures, influenced by Christianity and Islam, regard urine as unclean. However, the faiths and traditions that preceded these religions were far less averse to contact with bodily fluids, especially in eastern and southern cultures. Drinking urine as a health tonic is widely practiced by Hindus, for instance.

Finding ways in which urine has been used is easy. Mention the topic in any crowd and someone invariably relates an example from either personal experience or history. Scholarly references on this topic are sparse, but two books provide enlightenment. *The RE/Search Guide to Bodily Fluids* by Paul Spinrad (Juno Books, 1999) is an excellent addition to the bathroom bookshelf for its engaging reports on historical uses of bodily excretions, from menstrual blood to urine. Another is the encyclopedic *Scatologic Rites of All Nations* by John G. Bourke (W. H. Lowdermilk, 1891), which chronicles a long and detailed history of dung and urine use. The book's subtitle is almost a chapter in itself: "A Dissertation upon the Employment of Excrementitious Remedial Agents in Religion, Therapeutics, Divination, Witchcraft,

Love-Philters, etc. in all Parts of the Globe. Based upon Original Notes and Personal Observation, and upon Compilation from over One Thousand Authorities. Not for General Perusal." Not surprisingly, the German translation of the book, published in 1913, featured an introduction by Sigmund Freud, the father of psychoanalysis.

According to Bourke, many of the world's creation myths explain that the land, the oceans, and the first people were derived from the urine, feces, and menstrual blood of the gods. However, as cultures and religions were replaced by new powers and faiths, the revered myths and practices of the old were recast as the devils and taboos of the new. Carried forward to the 21st century, this leaves us with perhaps an overdeveloped aversion to excreta that is at odds with modern knowledge of bacteriology, disease risk, and wastewater management. The result is a limited and unbalanced view of life that denies essential aspects of both our bodies and the nutrient cycle—and perhaps hinders our development as human beings who fully understand and embrace the cycles and functions of life.

Whatever the case, a glimpse of the history of urine use is at once amusing, ironic, and enlightening.

Urine Conveniences

✿ In the French city of Versailles, women even urinated during church services; Louis Bourdaloue, a Jesuit preacher active there during the 17th century, delivered sermons so long that they inspired the invention of the "bourdaloue," an oblong porcelain vessel women congregants would use beneath their skirts.

✿ A professor of water and wastewater studies in Germany reports that some bars in southern Germany feature urinals built right into the bars, so patrons need not miss any drinking time when nature calls.

Urine to Dye for

✿ Urine has long been used instead of or as a substitute for alum, a dye fixer that helps the color better penetrate and adhere to fabric.

✿ BBC Radio 4 reports that in the late 19th century, Londoners could sell their urine for fixing dye. People could get about a penny a bucket, with redheads getting a half-penny more as their urine was particularly prized. Urine was ultimately credited with saving the textile industry. One might call that "trickle-down economics."

✿ In the United Kingdom, newly shorn wool was dipped in stale urine and rinsed. A more specific story has it that in parts of Scotland, woolen yarn was treated by soaking it in vats of urine before it was woven into tweed cloth.

❖ Some traditional European recipes produce blue, violet, and bluish red dyes from stale urine and lichens. Urine has been used to extract the blue color from indigo to dye blue jeans.

❖ Michael Braungart, renowned green chemist, relates the story of a German textile company that could not duplicate the fine color results of a dyer who had retired. Finally, after several substandard batches were produced, the retired employee was consulted. What was his secret? He admitted that, because he did not have toilet facilities nearby at night, he often used the dye vats as a urinal. The secret ingredient was identified.

Urine Cleaners

❀ Early Romans used urine as a tooth whitener and mouthwash.

❀ When water supplies were low, Mongolian horse warriors washed themselves in urine, which helped combat skin diseases such as crotch rot. "They smell so heavily that one cannot approach them," a Chinese traveler to Mongolia reported.

❀ Eskimos created steam baths by urinating on hot stones in an enclosed tent.

❀ One old Pennsylvania Dutch belief was that washing the face of a child with his or her own urine made the child good looking.

❀ Urine has also been used to bleach hair, cleanse teeth, clean clothes, and wash the body (particularly in cold climates).

❀ Some claim urine helps fade freckles.

❀ In the United Kingdom, clothing was washed in stale urine to kill lice and cut grease, perhaps thanks to urine's ammonia content.

Culinary Urine

❀ Chinook Indians prepared "Chinook olives" by soaking acorns in urine for five months.

❀ Before yeast was introduced, European bakers may have used urine in breadmaking.

❀ Cheesemakers in Germany and Switzerland used urine in their cheese. According to Bourke, a storekeeper in Berlin was punished for using the urine of young girls to make his cheese richer and more piquant, but people continued buying and enjoying it anyway.

❀ The Oxford English Dictionary's entry for "chamber lye" states that taverns extended cheap ale with urine; many jokes suggest that this practice continues to this day in the United States.

Urine Good Health

✿ Native Americans of New England treated ant and snake bites with pine pitch, human urine, and snakeroot. Today, applying urine is often recommended as an effective remedy for alleviating the pain of jellyfish stings.

✿ In Sweden, urine has been commonly used to clean wounds as well as ingested as a health tonic.

✿ Toilet manufacturers in Japan and England produce "smart toilets" that electronically analyze the toilet user's urine for sugar, protein, and urobilinogen. This data can be transmitted to a physician.

✿ Aztec physicians used urine to clean wounds to prevent infection, and administered it as a drink to relieve stomach problems.

✿ In old China, male urine was boiled down and the sludge on the side of the pot collected and rolled into pills touted to reinvigorate health. This may be due to the testosterone in the urine.

❁ Ancient physicians looked to urine for clues to their patients' maladies, examining it both visually and by tasting it. Hindu physicians diagnosed diabetes when a subject's urine tasted sweet. Another test was to put urine near an ant nest. If the ants ignored the urine, the patient was not diabetic. Urinanalysis continues today—by means other than tasting.

Urine in Wartime

❁ Using urine and other components, one can construct a urea nitrate explosive, commonly known as a "urine bomb."

❁ During the American Civil War, the women of Richmond, Virginia reportedly saved their urine for the manufacture of explosives.

❁ During World War I, soldiers without gas masks urinated on cloth and held it to their mouths and noses during a gas attack.

Urine Customs

❀ The Chukchi of Siberia and the English and Dutch of Elizabethan times independently practiced "drinking flapdragons," as the English called it, meaning toasting to someone's health by drinking a draught of urine. The Siberians used it to cement friendships, with the newly sworn allies drinking both their own and each others' urine.

❀ In Greenland and Iceland, people urinated at the dinner table into a chamber pot that servants (and sometimes the host's daughter) placed underneath the table when bidden.

❀ Medicine men in southern Africa sprinkled their urine on young newly married couples, while in northern Africa, the bride's urine was sprinkled on the guests. Among the Chukchi in northeastern Siberia, the bride and groom drank each other's urine. In England and Ireland the guests drank the bride's urine. Throughout Europe, there is an old custom of sprinkling the wedding guests with either the bride's bath water or the bride's urine. Another old European custom has the couple urinate through the wedding band shortly after the marriage to ward off bad luck. This custom has evolved to drinking a toast of an alcoholic beverage.

❀ Urination posture customs vary among cultures. Cultures where women stood and men sat or squatted were the Apaches, Mojaves, ancient Egyptians, aboriginal Australians, ancient Irish, and Maori (New Zealand). Turks sat; they considered it a heresy to urinate while standing because urine might sully their robes. The Angolans and Chinese stood, and some high-ranking Chinese men even urinated through hollow gold canes. Maori, Bedouin, and Apache men urinated while walking.

❀ At childbirth in France and Scotland, the mother's breasts were washed with a healthy man's urine. Similarly, both California natives and New England midwives would directly feed urine to newborns.

Ritual Urine

❀ Many Siberian, Nordic, Eskimo, and Native American cultures held what John Bourke calls "ur-orgies," religious or quasi-religious celebrations that employ urine. One example is the Urine Dance of the Zuñi (a Native American tribe) in which participants quaffed large urns of urine. The Zuñis claimed that medicine men organized these rites to adapt the participants' stomachs to a wide range of foods—perhaps a legacy of times when droughts necessitated extreme measures to get water.

❧ The aborigines of Queensland, Australia found that the nuts of a particular species of pine become psychoactive after fermenting in human urine.

❧ Urine figures in many rituals thanks to the hallucinogenic properties of the fly agaric mushroom (Amanita Muscaria—not to be confused with psilocybin mushrooms). This mushroom has been used for religious ceremonies in Siberia, Scandinavia, Lapland, and India since prehistoric times. The mushroom's hallucinogen passes through the body with its potency intact until about the seventh passing. The first ingestion reduces the mushroom's nausea-inducing effects. One source reports that in Danish Viking society, the mushroom was ingested by the strongest warrior, and his urine was then passed around to the others.

❧ Urine has been used in spells to ward off evil spirits. In early Britain, a witch bottle was buried in the hearth or in the wall over the home's entrance. This small bottle contained urine of the woman of the house in addition to pins or nails, which would cause severe bladder pain to any witch who tried to enter.

Utilitarian Urine

❧ According to ancient Egyptian medical texts, urine from a pregnant woman was added to small dishes filled with Nile mud and planted with seeds of wheat and seeds of barley; if the dish with the barley grew first, the woman could expect a boy; if the dish with the wheat grew first, then a girl would be born; if neither barley nor wheat dishes sprouted, the woman was not pregnant.

❧ Urine mixed with carbon dust has been used as a tattoo pigment.

❧ Soaking tobacco leaves in the urine of young girls was part of a traditional cigar manufacturing process in Cuba.

❀ Human and animal urine has been used in the manufacture of salt, phosphorus, saltpeter, and sal ammoniac.

❀ According to a report in *New Internationalist* magazine, urine is an insecticide, fertilizer, and pesticide for a village in Senegal, where they collect cow and human urine, "ferment" it for a few days, dilute it with water, and spray it over cotton plants. It repels white flies better than chemical pesticides. It also serves as a fertilizer, and its acidity kills newly emerging weeds.

❀ Eighteen months into explorer Ferdinand Magellan's voyage to circumnavigate the globe in 1519, the crew on his fleet of five ships ran out of fresh water and drank their own urine. Wrote one crewman, "It was surprisingly not unsavory, having no worse a taste than a flagon most foul with rancid port, as many I have tasted before."

❀ Urine was collected from community urinals in Pakistan and used to cure leather.

❀ In at least one Chinese city, collecting urine is big business. Urikinase, an enzyme derived from human urine, is used to dissolve blood clots.

❀ Two United States major league baseball players—a New York Yankees catcher and a Chicago Cubs outfielder—reportedly urinate on their hands to toughen them up during the baseball season. This is curious because urine contains urea, which is typically used as a softener.

Urine in Popular Culture

❀ In Sigmota, Sweden, "Pee Outside Day" was declared in 1999 to show that water can be saved by avoiding the needless flushing of urine.

❀ A Broadway musical comedy perhaps portends the future. The Tony Award-winning satire "Urinetown" is set in a city where a recent drought has reached such proportions that the play's characters must pay a fee to relieve themselves. A stereotypically evil corporation, UGC (Urine Good Company), has convinced the local government to outlaw private toilets in an effort to save water and gain a monopoly on public toilets. Residents caught breaking the law and urinating outside the public amenities are taken to the mysterious Urinetown. When UGC hikes the fee per use, riots ensue.

❀ Today, a black market for human urine provides drug-free urine for those attempting to pass drug tests.

❀ Before one of the wounded heroes in Dan Brown's thriller novel, *Deception Point,* must jump into an ocean full of sharks to escape his pursuers, he tapes his bleeding wounds and swaths his urine on his body to mask the smell of his blood from the hungry sharks. He recalls learning that "uric acid is the most potent-smelling fluid the human body made." The sharks leave him alone. He swims to safety and explains to his comrades, "Urine is the key!"

Urine Therapy

"Drink waters out of thine own cistern"
– Book of Proverbs

Urine therapy[1], or "urotherapy," is the practice of using urine to treat physical ailments—from jellyfish stings to sinus colds.

In fact, human urine has been used as a health tonic and cure throughout recorded history and most likely long before.

Today, books on the topic tout urine therapy as a remedy for such a wide range of ailments that it would seem to be a miracle cure for nearly any condition. There appears to be no well-controlled studies that show that urine therapy can cure life-threatening internal diseases, only anecdotal reports. However, some doctors acknowledge the antiseptic properties of urine, which may be effective for cleaning cuts and treating skin wounds, such as jellyfish stings.

Urine has been drunk by those with no access to reliable water during times of hardship (and is still done as an exercise in U.S. Army survival training) with no harmful effects. It is unlikely that drinking one's own urine will be harmful. Freshly secreted urine is usually sterile (except, for example, when the urinator has a urinary or kidney infection), and you can't give yourself an illness that you don't already have.

Urine is 95 percent water, with some salts and urea, as well as creatine and other minerals, hormones, and proteins. Although it is a waste product of the kidneys' filtration of bodily fluids, some of its components may offer valid benefits. There are several theories why.

Hormonal Value

As a health tonic, one theory is that urine—and morning urine in particular—contains high amounts of melatonin, a hormone produced by the body during the night. A hormone that helps regulate sleep, melatonin might make the body feel better rested than it actually is. Urine is also purported to contain a compound known as muramyl dipeptide, which mirrors the action of seratonin, a calming hormone.

Fertility drugs contain estrogens from human urine that stimulate

---

1. Urine therapy is presented here as an example of urine use. Its mention in this book is not an endorsement.

A Doctor Examining Urine by Trophîme Bigot (b. ca. 1600, Arles, d. 1650, Avignon). Ashmolean Museum, Oxford, England.

ovulation in women and sperm production in men. The estrogen-replacement drug for women, Premarin, is derived from mares' urine and other natural sources, including human urine.

Homeopathic Power

Another theory for the curative power of urine is the homeopathic one: When one digests one's own urine, the body reacts to its own physical condition reflected in the urine and produces a stronger immune response than it would otherwise. For example, cancer and other diseases release chemicals called antigens into the bloodstream. When the immune system detects them, it responds by producing antibodies to fight the invading disease. Some antigens produced by cancer cells appear in the urine, so practitioners hypothesize that if they give urine to cancer patients, the immune system will react more vigorously by producing a greater number of antibodies, thereby increasing its capacity to kill tumor cells.

Anticlotting Properties

While investigating historical anecdotes that drinking urine can prevent strokes and help break down blood clots, researchers found that a component of urine could digest proteins, specifically fibrin, the key in clotting. In 1952, a researcher isolated the anticlotting enzyme in urine and named it "urokinase." It is now used in preparations to break up clots in heart disease and strokes.

For cancer treatment, some urine therapy proponents maintain that urine inhibits the ability of cancer cells to stick together, which disrupts their nutrient intake and waste excretion, so they eventually die. Another claim is that some components in urine provide a biochemical defense system that prevents cancer from spreading.

As a health tonic, practitioners recommend: (1) Collecting urine in the morning when it is strongest, and (2) collecting it midstream to avoid the first flush of particles and sludges. Any rank taste or smell is generally due to diet: Coffee, alcohol, and spicy foods can give urine a sharp taste and odor. It is advised to ingest one's own urine only.

Antibacterial Agent

Doctors generally agree that urine can be a valid cleanser for wounds, especially when clean water is not available. As salty and nearly sterile water, urine may be one's best bet for cleansing a wound when there is no supply of clean water. It's also used to remedy stings, perhaps thanks to its urea content.

Urea is a recognized antibacterial, antifungal, and antiviral agent. The presence of urea in the urine is the result of the body's chemical balancing of a sodium chloride (salt) and water ratio. When used on a wound, urea causes an osmotic imbalance that kills bacteria and fungus. It is so effective it is used in many topical ointments and creams. Urea is found in medicines used to treat inflammation, including those for herpes infections. Urea is also a skin-softening ingredient in skin creams, although it is typically derived from nonhuman sources.

Although the thought of drinking one's urine is abhorrent to many Westerners, using urine as a healing agent has been practiced in many cultures for centuries. Can it be that our bodies excrete cures for their own ailments? Or is urine simply salty water with a trace of hormones and urea? Whether or not one uses it, it is clear that the properties of urine deserve consideration of their benefits.

Unexpected Urinals
Uncommon and Curious Urinals

Urinal Entertainment

The You're In Control game makes urination fun! Sensors in the back of a urinal detect the position of the urine stream, enabling users to play interactive games on a screen mounted above the urinal. The game was developed by Dan Maynes-Aminzade and Hayes Solos Raffle, students at the Massachusetts Institute of Technology's Media Lab.

(Above) A woman uses simulated urination (two water bottles and a hose fitted in a harness) to aim at the flying prairie dog depicted on the You're In Control screen (left) above the interactive urinal.

Urinal as Art

Fountain is a porcelain urinal that was part of a collection called "The Readymades." The artist Marcel Duchamp sought to challenge the notion of what was art. Duchamp half-seriously entered Fountain in a New York exhibit of avant garde artists under the name R. Mutt.

Duchamp wanted viewers of his work to see the beauty of common objects when removed from their everyday settings.

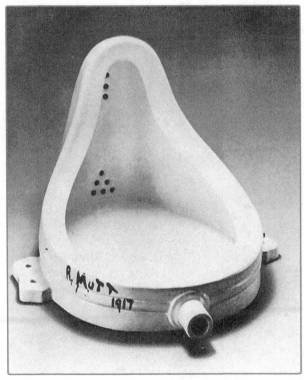

Fountain, by Marcel DuChamp, 1917
Philadelphia Museum of Art

Urinals for Women

Urinals for women are not new, but the demand for these has been limited.

Lately, women's urinals have popped up at music festivals where disposable cardboard personal urine diverters, such as the P-Mate (below), are provided with which to use them.

The advantage: More service in a smaller space and shorter waits for portable toilets.

photo: P-Mate

At left, the Urinette She-inal was designed by an American woman in the early 1990s, but this fixture never caught on. Most likely, women did not like using the urine-collection cup. This one is at a Dairy Queen restaurant in Florida.

The squat-over urinal enjoyed more popularity and was made until the 1960s for women to use standing or

squatting. This one is in the athletics building at Western Washington University in Bellingham, Wash. The flush knob is on the floor.

Today, the European "Lady P" by Sphinx offers a modern porcelain urinal for the ladies.

Urinals in Bloom

Ceramic artist Clark Sorensen's urinals in the shapes of flowers and shells have been exhibited at galleries worldwide. "I had the idea while standing over a urinal many times a day and letting the shape inspire me," he says. "The flower is the shape I chose partly because I love flowers and partly because it is the perfect contradiction: taking a mundane, even ugly object and transforming it into something beautiful."

The water flows differently in each design. "It really adds to the experience," he says "It's great to watch people react to flushing these urinals. It almost always brings out a smile and a giggle or more."

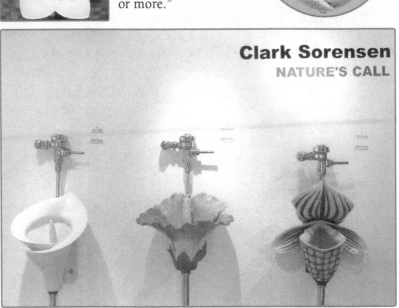

Clark Sorensen
NATURE'S CALL

Circumstantial Urinals

In the center of Reading, a town outside of London, stainless steel cylinders rise from the ground at 9 p.m. via a hydraulic motor.

The cyclinders are urinals installed for people to use at night after the pubs and clubs close. These units are manufactured by Urilift, a Dutch company.

Underground by day   *Above ground for night use*

The urinal in the Mir Space Station, which was in orbit around Earth for 15 years. Mir burned up in the earth's atmosphere in 2001. This mock-up of the station's fixtures is on display at Europa Park, a theme park located near Freiburg, Germany.

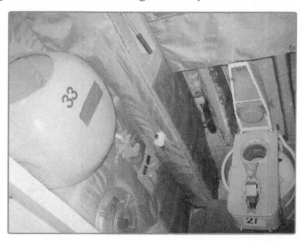

Activist's Urinal

This tree urinal is one of many scatologically themed cartoons by César Añorve, an architect and political cartoonist outside of Mexico City. Añorve, a water activist, seeks out and promotes solutions to the contaminated water and farmlands caused by water and wastewater mismanagement. To that end, he designs and promotes waterless toilet systems, which separate urine. However, to help get the public to talk about issues of excreta, he creates posters and booklets, such as *Psicoanalilis de la Zurrada* (from which this drawing is taken) that show this daily act in a humorous light.

See more about Añorve's work in the Gold to Green chapter.

Misplaced Urinals

According to a 2003 Associated Press story, one county highway cleanup crew in Washington state picked up 2,666 jugs of urine in one nine-month period, mostly around rest stops. The Adams County Waste Reduction & Recycling office took out a full-page newspaper advertisement and printed a poster announcing a $1,025 fine for dumping such waste. The problem is statewide.

In the future, truckers and other motorists can empty their urine jugs into urine composters, tanks, and specially designed garden beds installed at rest areas and other stops along highways. Then they may reuse the jugs.

Double-Duty Urinal

The combination sink and urinal saves water by using the drained washwater from the sink to flush the urinal beneath it. When the user washes his hands after using the urinal, the soapy water from the sink will flow down into the urinal thus cleaning it. This prototype was designed by Lee Jianxing of Singapore when he was 14. It won a design competition for youth sponsored by Sony. An Italian sanitary ware company now offers this combination fixture.

Similar fixtures are manufactured for toilets.

Interpretive Urinals

One of three fanciful urinals at the John Michael Kohler Arts Center in Sheboygan, Wisconsin. This one is in the men's room of The Social History of Architecture section of the building. New York artist Matt Nolen created this and two other urinals, as well as three sinks, two stalls, and wall art depicting changing architectural styles from ancient Egypt to current times. The restrooms at the Kohler Arts Center were featured on the Discovery Channel's program, *The World's Ten Best Bathrooms*.

Another men's room at the Kohler Art Center was created by artist Ann Agee. The walls depict the many places one sees water — from car washes and sewage plants to the shores of Lake Michigan and shelves of bottled water. This urinal features cobalt blue paisley-like protozoans one would see in a drop of water with a microscope.

Science and Technology
of Using Liquid Gold

Why Manage Urine Separately?

Many individuals and communities worldwide are diverting and using urine for several reasons:

❀ In wastewater, urine accounts for most of the nutrients—as much as 90 percent of the nitrogen and potassium.

❀ These nutrients can get into groundwater and lakes, rivers, and streams where they can pollute by overfertilizing aquatic plants.

❀ Oxidized and diluted, urine makes a good nutrient for plants.

❀ Several studies validated the collection and use of urine to fertilize crops, such as wheat, corn, and oats. (Jonsson, 1997; Winblad, 1997)

❀ Urine is usually sterile in healthy populations.

❀ Urine is portable and easy to collect separately and drain away.

❀ Urine mixed with feces produces a malodorous compound—worse than each of its components alone. (Wolgast, 1993)

However, collecting and using urine presents some challenges:

❀ The urea in urine degrades rapidly to the gasses ammonia and carbon dioxide unless it is contained or directly utilized. (Sundberg, 1995)

❀ Urine contained without air will smell bad.

Urine, the Pollutant

The nutrients in urine can cause overgrowth of aquatic plants in lakes, rivers, and streams. When they die and decompose, they use up oxygen in the water, which suffocates other aquatic life such as fish. This is called hypoxia. (See Broken Nutrient Cycle and Closed Nutrient Cycle, pages 42 and 43.)

When it gets into drinking water supplies, nitrogen can result in such diseases as methaemoglobimaemia, or "blue baby syndrome." To protect public health, the U.S. Safe Drinking Water Act now requires communities to reduce the nitrogen in wastewater, which often requires expensive denitrification equipment.

The Fertilizer Value of Urine

In one year, the average northern European adult produces 116 gallons of urine. Many studies give the average daily nitrogen output for a healthy adult at about 11 grams. That figure ranges widely, mostly depending on diet. The more plant or animal protein the population eats, the more nitrogen it excretes. (Ralf Otterpohl, 1998)

Two Swedish university studies report that one northern European adult (who consumes plant and animal proteins) produces enough fertilizer in urine to grow 50 to 100 percent of the food requirement for another adult. We excrete these nitrogen-containing compounds as urea, creatine, ammonia, and a small amount of uric acid. These nutrients could feed a hungry and growing population at a lower cost than producing more expensive chemical fertilizer. (Sundberg, 1995; Drangert, 1997)

The world needs all the nutrients we are flushing away each day in our urine. Given the far-reaching costs of using manufactured fertilizers, utilizing this valuable and usually sterile resource deserves more consideration. Urine costs nothing to produce (unless you count the plant and animal protein we eat), but it does have storage and transportation costs, as does commercial chemical fertilizer.

Keeping Urine Separate

Our bodies keep urine separate naturally, so we can collect and use it separately. Urine-diverting toilets, which feature a urine collector and drain are cast into the front of the toilet bowl opening, make urine collection as easy as using a flush toilet.

How to Use It

To use urine for fertilizer, it must be oxidized to a form that plants can use called nitrate. Or it can be diluted and mixed into well-aerated soil, where the soil's aerobic microbes complete the oxidation (nitrification) process.

Using urine right away is best. If it is exposed to air for a while, the nitrogen starts to change into ammonia gas and

Urine-diverting toilets and urinals in a display room in Sweden.

waft away. (Nitrogen is an essential part of our atmosphere; it's what makes the sky blue.)

To oxidize or compost it (some erroneously call this "fermenting," an anaerobic process), the urine must be applied to carbon to create a carbon-to-nitrogen ratio (C:N) of one part urine to 25 parts carbon. This is the preferred diet of fast-acting aerobic bacteria that can convert all the nitrogen to nitrates. Easy ways to do that are: (1) Apply it to healthy soil with plenty of humus which contains lots of carbon (indicated by rotting leaves and roots and a nice crumbly texture—not sandy or dusty—and an earthy smell). (2) Compost it with high-carbon materials such as dry leaves, woodchips, and sawdust. (3) Combine it with gray-water (the water drained from sinks, tubs, and washing machines), which contains lots of water and a little bit of carbon.

Diverting and using urine may seem on the "lunatic fringe" now, but the benefits are so great that it will be a common sense practice in the future.

Composition of Daily Urine Normally Produced by an Adult

Substance	Amount
Urea	6.0–180 grams (nitrogen)
Creatine	0.3–0.8 gram (nitrogen)
Ammonia	0.4–1.0 gram (nitrogen)
Uric acid	0.008–0.2 gram (nitrogen)
Sodium	2.0–4.0 grams
Potassium	1.5–2.0 grams
Calcium	0.1–0.3 gram
Magnesium	0.1–0.2 gram
Chloride	4.0–8.0 grams
Phosphate	0.7–1.6 grams (phosphorus)
Inorganic sulfate	0.6–1.8 gram (sulfur)
Organic sulfate	0.006–0.2 gram (sulfur)

Source: *Van Nostrand's Scientific Encyclopedia*

Carbon Matching for the Hardcore Urine User

The two bacteria most responsible for converting urea into a nitrate are Nitrobacter and Nitrosomonas. These nitrifying bacteria need carbon for their protoplasm, their cell walls, and the enzymes that convert organic nitrogen molecules to nitrates. For a more specific inoculant, you can grow a Nitrobacter-Nitrosomonas culture by mixing urine and sugar, letting it process aerobically, and adding this to the urine barrel or composter.

The Carbon-Nitrogen Connection

Remember that the C:N ratio of urine (0.8:1) is too low for microbes to use and fully break down into a plant-usable form. To preserve all the fertilizer value of urine, a carbon-to-nitrogen ratio of 25:1 is need-ed to convert all the nitrogen to nitrates by aerobic soil bacteria. (Again, nitrate is the form of nutrient that plants use best.)

But that would require loads of high-carbon materials such as wood chips, peat moss, etc. Most of us are not on a farm that could provide enough straw or leaves from trees for this purpose. Instead of adding a room full of sawdust (C:N 400:1) to a year's worth of urine to achieve a C:N of 25:1, consider adding some more concentrated forms of carbon, such as alcohol (as wastewater treatment plants do) or simply sugar.

Why add sugar to a urine composter? Sugars are the most available of the carbohydrates and can provide a lot of carbon with little volume compared to straw, leaves, and woodchips. These are primarily diffi-cult-to-digest celluloses and lignin, which, in a composter, are decom-posed by fungi and actinomycetes, not by bacteria.

Sugar, however, is a simple carbohydrate. Adding some cane sugar may not seem ecologically elegant, but it will surely adjust the C:N ratio, in place of a truckload of sawdust. About a third of a cup of sugar per person per day should do it.

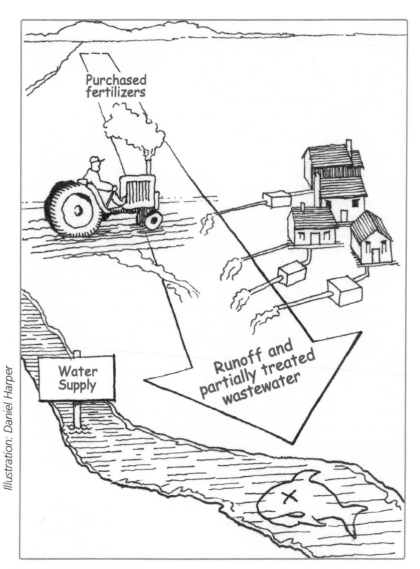

Illustration: Daniel Harper

Broken Nutrient Cycle

The nitrogen from wastewater, as well as from excess fertilizer, can leach into groundwater or lakes, rivers, and streams where it can be polluting. At the same time, farmers, landscapers, and plant nurseries purchase and apply nitrogen fertilizer, much of it artificially produced.

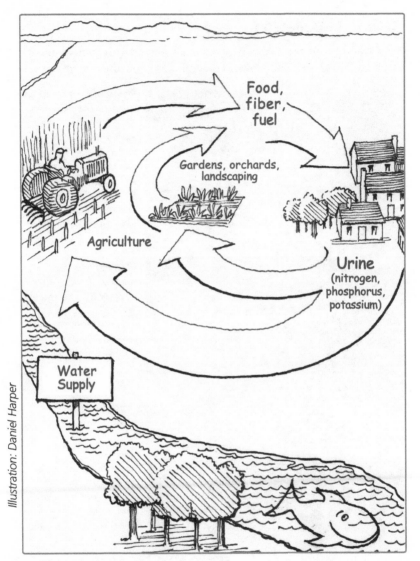

Illustration: Daniel Harper

Closed Nutrient Cycle
When we use the nitrogen in our wastewater—most of which is from human urine—to fertilize either farms or landscapes and gardens closer to its source, we recycle nutrients instead of polluting our waters. We also save the cost of buying and transporting nitrogen fertilizer.

Seeing Is Believing

Urine-use advocate Peter Morgan experiments with using diluted urine as fertilizer in Zimbabwe. These photos show the dramatic results.

Planters full of chard and spinach: The planter on the left was fertigated with a 3:1 mixture of water and urine. The planter on the right was fed with water only. Thanks to its high nitrogen content, urine is an especially good fertilizer for leafy greens.

Corn requires high volumes of nitrogen. The planter on the left was fertigated with a urine-water mixture while the one on the right was only watered.

The largest ears of corn on the left were fed a 3:1 water-urine mixture three times a week. The others were fed far less.

NASA Proves the Value of Liquid Gold

NASA (National Aeronautics and Space Administration) in the United States conducted the first controlled studies of using human waste as a hydroponic nutrient solution for growing food plants in the 1970s and '80s.

"Urine is approximately 95% water, 2.5% urea, and 2.5% contains a mixture of minerals and organic substances such as hormones, amino acids, enzymes, etc. When properly diluted with water, urine makes an excellent fertilizer." To demonstrate, NASA scientists grew vegetables such as cherry tomatoes and string beans using a hydroponic solution of 0.5% urine and tap water. It was pumped through the plants' roots for 15 minutes every hour. After about four months, the cherry tomatoes had produced an average of 210 tomatoes per vine with a total plant height of about 11 feet (3.4 m). Domestic wastewater was also tested. The study found that the plants cleaned the wastewater, removing or reducing several constituents.

– Growing Clean Water by Bill Wolverton

Nitrogen-loving leafy greens, such as this spinach, respond dramatically to diluted urine.

The spinach on the left was watered with diluted urine. The spinach on the right was irrigated with water only.

The City as Fertilizer Factory

It's conceivable that the urine produced by a city could fertilize all the food it requires, according to Dr. Jan-Olof Drangert, a professor at Linköping University in Sweden. Cities can serve as nutrient batteries that power the farms that surround them, as has been done throughout history, he says (*Perceptions, Urine Blindness and Urban Agriculture*, 1997).

China has a long history of collecting and using mixed excreta to fertilize farms, Drangert reports. "Japan imported this tradition in the 12th century, and farmers bought urine and feces from town dwellers. When cheap chemical fertilisers became available, the Japanese farmers switched to those, and the town councils had to solve the arising sanitation problem partly with sewers." Up to today, half of the excreta in Japan is collected by municipalities and used for agricultural purposes.

Densely populated cities may have insufficient open land to use all urine, so it must be transported to farms in outlying areas. There are several formulas for figuring the land area needed to grow away urine, and variables range widely. Drangert's general equation: "Vegetation on some 50 to 100 m2 (164 to 328 square feet) may be enough to consume the nutrients from the urine of one person if intensive agriculture is practiced with three crops a year.... One adult eats 250 kg (551 lbs) of cereals per year, which has been grown on less than 500 m2 (1640 square feet) and fertilized to 50 percent by the person's urine."

In cities and towns with more open space, urine can be used within the city. Drangert figures that, with more than 656 to 984 square feet (200 to 300 square meters) of open space per person, the

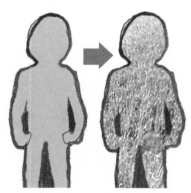

Two Swedish university studies report that one northern European adult (who consumes plant and animal proteins) produces enough fertilizer in urine to grow 50 to 100 percent of the food requirement for another adult (variables include climate, crop requirements, soils, and diet of the urine contributors).

Illustration by César Añorve

Urine, written in many languages, adds up to "NPK," the nitrogen-phosphorus-potassium content ratio of fertilizers. The average NPK of urine is about 11-1-2.5 in a western population.

opportunity to grow away all the urine is greater even without intensive agriculture. With more than half of the world's population expected to live in cities over the next two decades, this nutrient equation might be a critical one for assuring a sustainable food supply.

Diverting Urine Saves Money

In a Dutch town, water researcher Dr. Jac Wilsenach calculated that if just half of the town's urine were diverted from all wastewater, the treatment plant could treat nearly all the nitrogen and phosphorus without an energy-intensive denitrification or "polishing" stage. Also, lower starting levels of these nutrients allow microbes in the aeration tanks to do their job much more efficiently, thus reducing the energy demand—a significant cost savings. What's more, the resulting sludge is richer in organic matter and generates more than three times more methane. —*Journal of Environmental Engineering*, Vol. 132

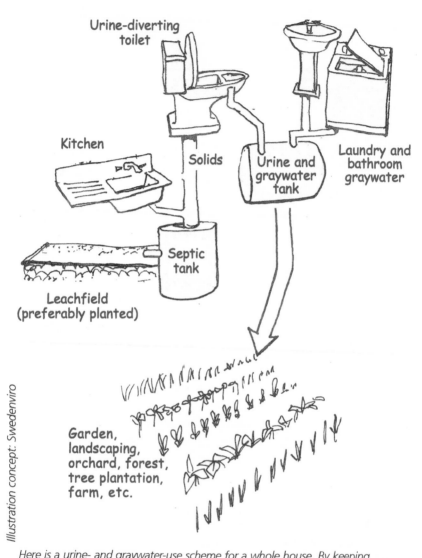

Urine-diverting toilet

Kitchen

Solids

Urine and graywater tank

Laundry and bathroom graywater

Septic tank

Leachfield (preferably planted)

Garden, landscaping, orchard, forest, tree plantation, farm, etc.

Illustration concept: Swedenviro

Here is a urine- and graywater-use scheme for a whole house. By keeping graywater (washwater) and urine separate from feces and kitchen sink wastes (which could contain blood from meat), the effluents with the most value and least disease risk are utilized.

How to Use Urine Safely

Whenever we grow food crops with wastewater, there is a potential health risk. Fortunately, as stated before, urine is usually sterile in healthy populations. It is also important to remember that you cannot infect yourself with diseases you do not have.

Precautions for Your Health

According to sanitation researcher Caroline Schönning of the Swedish Institute of Infectious Disease Control, humans rarely excrete disease-causing organisms, or *pathogens*, in urine. Also, most pathogens die when they leave their hosts, either immediately or shortly thereafter. The only significant urine-transmitted diseases are leptospirosis (usually transmitted by infected animals), schistosoma, and salmonella. The first two are rare—usually found only in tropical aquatic environments—and the last is typically inactivated shortly after excretion. The more likely health risk is urine contaminated by feces that were misplaced in a urine-diverting toilet.

Ways to inactivate pathogens include time (waiting them out), composting, heat, and adding high-alkaline additives such as lime and wood ash. Here are some general guidelines for use:

✿ For inactivation of most pathogens that may be present, especially if urine from outside of your household has been collected to fertilize food crops, store urine for six months before use. This period can be shortened if the ambient temperature is higher, such as 65 degrees. For lowest risk usage, apply it to crops that do not touch the earth, such as orchard fruit, vines, and berry bushes. Or use it only for crops that will be cooked or fed to animals. When in doubt, don't use it.

✿ For personal and household urine used for growing food, Schönning deems it an acceptable health risk to allow one month to pass after urine-fertilization before harvesting crops that are eaten raw.

✿ Urine is best worked into the soil or applied under the soil to reduce exposure, allow soil organisms to deactivate pathogens, and preserve its nutrient value.

Precautions for Plant Health

Growing plants with urine is simple, but it does require some know-how. Pouring undiluted urine on dirt can result in odors, lost nutrients, unbalanced soils, and dead plants. It's important to remember:

❁ Use urine as you would any soil amendment: Be sure the amendment meets the needs of the plants you are cultivating.

❁ Urine can be salty, so use it where there is good drainage and where rainwater will flush it out occasionally. Or, use salt-uptaking plant varieties such as salt cedar to remove salts every few years.

❁ Urine is acidic. Add a little wood ash or a light application of lime especially if you are growing alkaline-loving plants.

❁ Urine continuously applied to the same spot can overwhelm plants with too much nitrogen. Dilute and distribute it.

Three Ways to Grow Away Urine

To use urine safely to fertilize plants for minimal odors and maximum nutrient use:

❁ Compost it.

❁ Combine it with graywater (washwater) in an aerobic garden bed.

❁ Dilute and apply it directly to plants.

Compost It

Pour urine into a composter full of lots of carbon materials (brown leaves and garden clippings, sawdust, wood shavings, untreated bark chunks, shredded paper, cardboard, etc.).

You can use an enclosed composter, an open composter, or a bin with drainage holes. Urine adds moisture and nitrogen that carbon materials need to decompose faster.

Remember that food scraps and green yard wastes already contain lots of nitrogen, so do not add much urine to composters with a high content of these materials.

Leaf composters can be made of chicken wire, snow fence, wooden pallets, or scrap wood. Plastic composters can be purchased from garden centers. Some municipalities offer them at a discounted price. Plant flowers or crops around the composter to use up any moisture (sometimes called "compost tea") that drains from the bottom of the composters.

Combine It with Graywater (Washwater) in an Aerobic Garden Bed

Graywater—the water that drains from sinks, showers, tubs, and washing machines—is a great addition to urine for plant use. Urine contains nitrogen. Graywater is a lot of water with a little carbon. The two combine well: The graywater dilutes the urine and its carbon content complements urine's nitrogen, so the mixture provides an ideal diet for the beneficial bacteria that transform the nitrogen to feed plants.

The graywater-urine mix is best drained to an aerobic graywater system filled with media that provides air pockets where fast-acting aerobic bacteria and plant roots work together.

In some areas, a wastewater permit may be required to install this system. Note: Most wastewater regulations will view urine the same as combined wastewater, despite its lower pathogen risk.

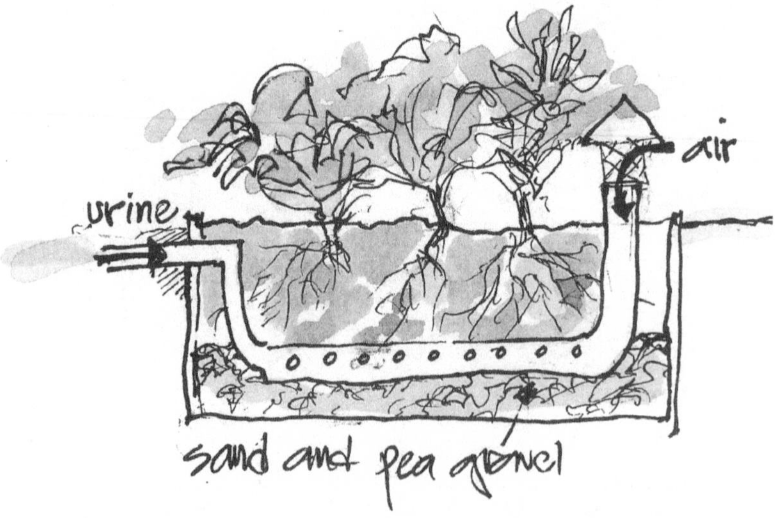
urine
air
sand and pea gravel

This graywater system is based on the Washwater Garden™. (Plans for it are available from Ecowaters Projects. See the end of this book.) It is a planted evapotranspiration system comprised of layers of 3/4-inch to 3-inch gravel, peastone, and sand. Other aerobic constructed ecosystems for wastewater can work too. (Because urine is salty, salt buildup is possible. Be sure to design the system so that rain and snow flushes it out. Or plant it with salt-loving plants.)

Dilute It and Apply It Directly to Plants

For direct application:

✿ Dilute the urine with at least eight parts water to one part urine (8:1).

✿ Or, pour urine only on well-mulched aerated soil. Soil covered with three inches of woodchips, untreated bark mulch, or leaf mulch and containing plenty of humus will withstand additions of undiluted urine.

A urine-diverting toilet that drains to a urine tank into which pressurized water dilutes it for application to plants is an easy way to use urine once you set it up. You can also collect urine in any container, such as a jug, and manually dilute it before applying it to plants.

Other Possibilities

There are other ways to use liquid gold. For small amounts of urine, you can make a urine planter. Layer shredded cardboard or paper with chunky sand or peastone. Add more material when the contents shrink as the paper decomposes. Plant hearty nutrient-loving plants, shrubs, or small trees. Urine also works well in hydroponic planter systems.

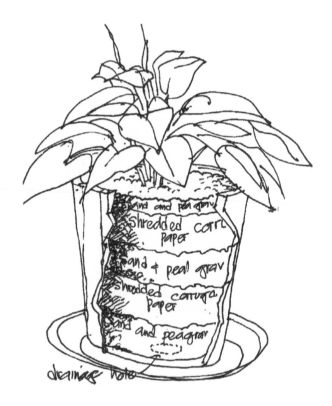

Layer sand and peastone with shredded cardboard in a planter to create a urine planter. Over time, the mix will decompose into a soil.

How to Keep Urine Separate

Fortunately, urine comes out of the human body separately, so collecting urine is as simple as directing that stream.

That can be as simple as urinating directly into a container (remember to use one with at least a two-cup capacity unless you are good at turning on and off the "faucet") or into a funnel that drains to a bottle. Men can use urinals. Whatever works.

There are also special toilets designed to divert urine. Urine-diverting toilets—also called urine-separating and no-mix toilets—differ from ordinary toilets in that they have two drains: a cup in the front of the bowl to collect and drain urine and a rear drain for feces and toilet paper.

The design and the flushing mechanism vary among models and manufacturers. Some flush urine and feces separately, some flush just urine (feces drop to a tank), and some are completely dry, relying on gravity. Urine flows through a pipe, separate from the solids—usually to a tank, where it is collected by a pump truck, much like a septic hauler's truck.

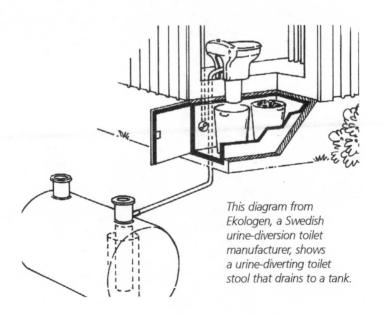

This diagram from Ekologen, a Swedish urine-diversion toilet manufacturer, shows a urine-diverting toilet stool that drains to a tank.

Urinals

Urinals are an easy way to divert (mostly male) urine in a conventional bathroom. The flush water even helps dilute the urine for use but it's not critical. In recent years, waterless urinals that require no flushing have entered the market. Many use special oil-seal traps to prevent odors.

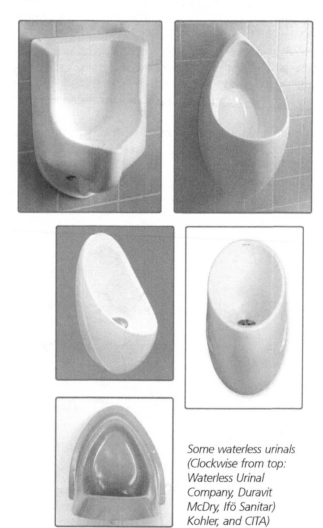

Some waterless urinals (Clockwise from top: Waterless Urinal Company, Duravit McDry, Ifö Sanitar) Kohler, and CITA)

Mr. PeeBuddy, a Low-Cost Make-It-Yourself Urinal

Mr. PeeBuddy was created by sailboat-liveaboard Chris Melo to reduce the load on his boat's holding tank. Made of plastic bottles and some gizmos found at most hardware stores, it features a stopcock (shut-off valve) and easy-to-use screw-off cap to make using and emptying it easy and odor free.

You'll need:

- A one-gallon plastic bottle to serve as a urinal
- A one-gallon bottle, such as a spring water bottle, for a storage bottle
- Two 1/2-in. nylon hose fittings*
- One 9/16-in. stopcock*
- 3 ft. of 1/2-in. plastic tubing or hose

1. Cut the one-gallon plastic bottle so it is the shape shown at right [A]. This is your urinal.

2. Drill or cut a 1/2-in. hole in the center of the caps of the urinal bottle and the storage bottle. Insert a 1/2-in. nylon hose fitting* in each hole.

3. Cut a 4-in. length of the 1/2-in. tubing or hose and attach between the urinal's hose fitting and the stopcock [B]. (You might need to heat the tubing so it will stretch and slip over the fittings.)

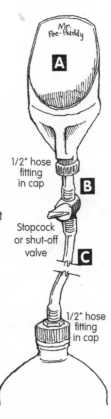

1/2" hose fitting in cap **B**

Stopcock or shut-off valve **C**

1/2" hose fitting in cap

4. Attach the urinal on the wall and place the storage bottle on the floor beneath the urinal. Measure the distance between the base of the stopcock and the hose fitting [C]. Cut a length of the tubing to fit. Attach it to the fitting and stopcock.

Optional: Cut a 3-in. daisy shape out of the plastic you cut out of the bottle, and place it in the drain to prevent items falling in.

Keep the stopcock closed when the urinal is not in use. Open it before use. This keeps odor in the bottle.

*The stopcock and hose fittings are available from U.S. Plastic: www.usplastic.com.

Waterless Urine-Diverting Toilets

Waterless urine-diverting toilets drain urine with gravity. Some models offer a one tablespoon "flush." Feces drop by gravity to holding tanks or composting systems. Feces kept separate can be dried (with additions of wood ash or lime) or composted (sometimes requiring added water and aeration).

Top: The porcelain Ekologen ES drains urine with or without a tablespoon of water.

Left: A fiberglass urine-diverting toilet stool used with drying toilet systems in Mexico by Centro de Innovacion en Tecnología Alternativa (CITA).

Below: A concrete vault system from CITA and plastic bins used with Ekologen toilet stools.

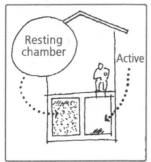

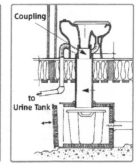

Some self-contained models divert urine and hold the solids in a container inside for composting, burning, or disposal.

In the Separett Villa, a plate over the solids container moves away when the user sits on the toilet, so the contents cannot be seen.

The Air Head Marine Composting Head is a small urine-diverting composting toilet made just for boats.

Other urine-diverting composting toilets include the Kiwi Bog, Naturum, and Cotuit Dry Toilet

Urine-Diverting Flush Toilets

Urine-diverting flush toilets flush urine with a small amount of water and feces with more water. Some flush with a vacuum assist.

The Dubbletten (left) and Ekologen DS (center) urine-diverting flush toilets from Sweden. The Roediger (right) from Germany is a vacuum-assist toilet.

Urine Diverters

Urine diverters range from inserts that fit into latrines and composting toilets to personal diverters that direct urine to its best use.

The Separett Privy Kit urine diverter

A funnel is an easy diverter/urinal. To keep odors and nitrogen inside the jug, place a ping pong ball in the opening of a shallow funnel. The ball will lift when urine enters the funnel.

Personal Diverters

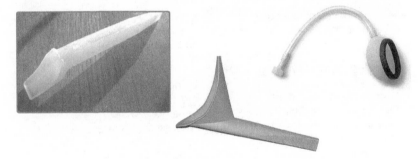

Who says a woman can't write her name in the snow? The Travelmate, Whiz Freedom, and Pisstazia help women direct urine into a container or even a urinal.

Sometimes the manual way is the simplest. Half-quart yogurt containers make great urine collectors.

Sources

Urine-Diverting Flush Toilets

Dubbletten (Sweden)
www.dubbletten.nu

Wost Man Ecology AB (Sweden)
www.wost-man-ecology.se
Manufacturer of Ekologen toilets

Ecovita (North America)
www.ecovita.net
Ekologen toilets

Gustavsberg (Sweden)
www.gustavsberg.com
Manufacturer of water-flush urine-diverting toilets

Roediger Vacuum Toilet (Germany)
www.roevac.de

Waterless Urine-Diverting Toilets

Centro de Innovación en Tecnología Alternativa (Mexico)
www.laneta.apc.org/esac/citaesp.htm
CITA fiberglass urine-diverting toilets and urinals

Separett (Sweden)
www.separett.com
Separett waterless urine-diverting toilets

Ecovita (North America)
www.ecovita.net
Separett, CITA, Air Head, and Ekologen urine-diverting toilets and urinals

Cotuit Dry Toilets (North America)
www.cape.com/cdt

Kiwi Bog Toilets (New Zealand)
www.kiwibog.com

Waterless Urinals

Ifö (Sweden)
www.ifosanitar.com
Manufacturer

Waterless Company
www.waterless.com
Manufacturer

Falcon Waterfree Technologies
www.falconwaterfree.com
Manufacturer

Uridan
www.uridan.com
Manufacturer

Ecovita USA
www.ecovita.net
Supplier

Urine Diverters

Separett (Sweden)
www.separett.com

Ecovita (North America)
www.ecovita.net

Personal Urine Diverters

P-Mate
www.p-mate.com

Whiz Freedom
www.whizaway.com

Travelmate (North America)
www.travelmateinfo.com
Personal urine diverter

Gold to Green
Profiles of Liquid Gold at Work in Gardens and Farms Worldwide

Photos: Verna Ecology

Urine is applied to a field with a liquid fertilizer application apparatus before planting.

Farming with Liquid Gold in Sweden

A tank truck pulls up to a housing development outside Stockholm, extends a hose into an underground tank. Later, the truck heads to a farm where its contents are discharged into storage tanks. Just a few months later, the tanks' contents—sanitized human urine—are pumped into a liquid fertilizer truck and applied to spring barley.

Sweden, awash with lakes and nearly surrounded by shoreline, is acutely aware of the fate of its wastewater and nutrients. The Baltic Sea is rife with eutrophication from nutrient-rich runoff.

In the late 1990s, the Stockholm Water Company and other agencies tested and proved the viability of using urine as an agricultural fertilizer. Urine-diverting toilets that flush with a small volume of water were installed in four housing projects, from an ecovillage with 44 apartments to a public housing development with 51 apartments. Urine was drained to in-ground fiberglass tanks. Then it was transported to a facility outside Stockholm for testing. A farmer used the tested urine to fertilize grain crops.

In Sweden, urine-diverting toilets have long been manufactured, primarily for vacation and mobile homes. About 3,000 porcelain urine-diverting toilets were sold there in the 1990s alone. However, they are less common in year-round homes, with the exception of ecologically oriented housing often called ecovillages.

The Swedish study found urine is almost equal in strength and effectiveness to liquid mineral fertilizers that farmers buy and use. Compared to animal manure, human urine lacks only the organics—carbon, fibers, and beneficial microorganisms. The study also

Grain crops were fertilized with urine in Swedish studies.

reported urine and flush water is free of pathogens if stored above freezing for three to six months. Naturally rising pH (from 7 to 9), high temperature, and time kill any pathogens present (from fecal contamination in the toilet).

The urine could also be used in gardens and landscapes at the housing developments.

The study is important for showing the significant advantages of collecting and using urine to enrich soils. Most conventional wastewater plants produce sewage sludge as a byproduct, and this is applied to forests and fields. However, sludge usually contains little nutrient content. Nitrogen and phosphorus are often reduced in conventional wastewater systems and discharged to where they can pollute. Urine diversion makes it possible to use them to fertilize farmland, turning a wastewater challenge into an opportunity.

Results of this study is detailed in the report, "Urine Separation— Closing the Nutrient Cycle." It also describes specifics of toilet installation, user acceptability, and farming techniques.

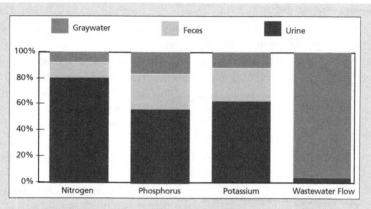

"The nitrogen (N), phosphorus (P) and potassium (K) in wastewater can be utilized instead of artificial fertilizer.... Recirculating nutrients from wastewater as fertilizer reduces the need of industrially produced fertilizer and also reduces discharges of nutrient-rich water from treatment plants into watercourses. Most of the nutrients that are essential in agriculture (N, P, K) occur in urine. Faeces contain smaller amounts of these substances, while the quantities in greywater are insignificant. Separating urine, which only accounts for about 1 percent of the total wastewater flow, and using it as fertilizer makes it possible to utilize most of the nutrient content of waste-water. If faecal matter is separated, too, only small amounts of nutrients remain in the greywater."

— Urine Separation—Closing the Nutrient Cycle

Liquid Gold for Phosphorus

In the Netherlands, the environmental services firm Grontmij trucks col-lected urine to a treatment plant where the phosphorus content is pre-cipitated out as a mineral called struvite (ammonium magnesium phos-phate). This common phosphorus-based soil amendment can help reduce demand for phosphate, which is usually mined, refined, and trucked to farms, using lots of energy. Some estimates suggest the world's phosphate mines will be exhausted in 100 years. Yet today we literally pour tons of perfectly good phosphate down the drain.

Quick Facts About Using Urine for Farm Fertilizer

❀ Human urine is a quick-acting fertilizer that can replace mineral fertilizer in cereal crop production. In trials, cereal crops fertilized with urine yielded 80 to 90 percent as much as those fertilized with mineral fertilizer.

❀ Nitrogen in urine is volatile; it can be lost to the air. So it must be stored in a covered container and worked into the soil to minimize nitrogen losses.

❀ Plants fertilized with urine suffered no toxic effects in trials. However, it's best not to fertilize seeded grassland, as urine may be too strong for sprouting seeds.

❀ An estimated 1.5 to 2.6 quarts (1.5 to 2.5 liters) of urine solution (yellow water) per person is produced daily.

❀ Urine can be transported up to 137 miles (220 km) before the energy used surpasses that of conventional treatment.

❀ Nitrogen losses in the form of ammonia were less than 10% of the nitrogen applied and usually much lower.

❀ The risk of nitrogen leaching into water is no greater than when mineral fertilizer is used.

Keeping a Lake Clean Outside Stockholm

Gebers is a former hospital next to a lake outside Stockholm, Sweden that was renovated into a 32-unit condominium building. To preserve the lake, the residents use Ekologen urine-diverting toilets.

Urine drains to two large polyethylene tanks in the basement pumped out periodically by a local farmer to fertilize grain crops. Solids drop to roll-away composter containers in the basement. When a composter is full, it is disconnected and moved to a finishing area in the corner of the cellar. After a year, it is emptied outside and composted further before it is applied to flower gardens.

Urine-diverting toilets drain to tanks in the basement. The urine is pumped out for use on grain crops. Below: Full feces composters are disconnected to complete their processing in the basement.

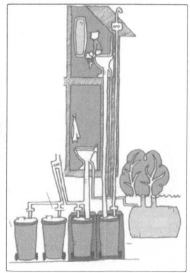

Anna Edey amidst plants fertilized with diluted urine at her home on Martha's Vineyard, an island off Massachusetts.

Photos: Anna Edey and Carol Steinfeld

Liquid Gold on Martha's Vineyard

Anna Edey has been using urine to nourish plants for more than 30 years. She is perhaps best known for her "biointensive" greenhouse that brimmed with life in nearly every square inch. Salad mix and other greens grew in trays, and chickens and rabbits in cages along the walls ate scraps and helped warm the greenhouse. She chronicled her experiences, experiments, and revelations in her inspirational book, *Solviva*.

Long before many researchers were documenting the nutrient value of urine, Anna had investigated the feasibility of using urine for fertilizer. "It truly surprised me when I discovered that this substance, so taboo and polluting in our society, is actually an excellent fertilizer," she says. "'You're-in-charge' began to put me in charge of my destiny."

Anna learned about using urine after she and her three daughters moved to a remote cottage with no indoor plumbing. Anna and her daughters used an outdoor pit latrine for a toilet, but they urinated in a pot in the house. This urine was diluted with water about 10:1 and poured around the yard.

The following spring, the effects of that practice manifested in a profusion of wild plants as well as cultivated ones that sprang forth much healthier than the previous year. She also noticed plants blooming longer than before. Indian poke plants grew 10 feet tall. Lush patches of spirea, St. Johnswort, Queen Anne's lace, and black-eyed Susan surrounded her cottage—where her family had poured the diluted urine.

"Most intriguing of all was the kinship and communication I sensed with these plants," she says. "The waste molecules from my body were being absorbed as nutrients by the living plants. I felt reincarnated while I was still alive. This liquid soon inspired new names: Peace-on-Earth. Urine-charge. You're-in-harmony. Aqua Vitae."

Anna learned through trial and error when to fertilize with urine and when not to, especially with potted plants. When green leaves start to turn yellow, the plant needs more nitrogen. When greens turn blueish and show a subtle shrinking, the plant is getting more than it needs.

Anna uses only diluted urine to fertilize the abundant fruits and vegetables she grows. At one point, she grew 200 full-grown onions in one square yard, fertilizing only with urine. (She emphasizes that she did not use it to grow vegetables for sale, because public perception of this practice would not allow it.) Anna also uses wood ash, which is alkaline, to balance the pH of urine, which is slightly acidic, and to supply extra potassium to plants.

Anna calls urine "peace-on-Earth, urine-charge, you're-in-harmony, and aqua vitae."

She observed that urine acts like chemical fertilizer when fed to plants directly but does not supply the full spectrum of nutrients and materials that provide structure and diverse life to soil. To achieve that, she adds compost, a biologically rich mix of decomposed food scraps, leaves, and yard clippings. Compost provides a diverse soil biota that helps plants fend off diseases, convert nutrients for use, and helps the soil hold water and air. She also pours urine into her compost bin to speed the decomposition process.

Photos: Arne Backlund, www.backlund.dk

A garden allotment shed in Denmark

Gardeners' Toilets in Denmark

In parts of Scandinavia, many city dwellers rent little garden plots called "allotments" just outside their cities. These are often 20-by-20-foot garden plots where renters build tiny sheds for tools, chairs, personal items, and, occasionally, toilets. Most of these toilets are chemical, but some are composting.

In one area in Denmark, urine-diverting toilets were offered to allotment owners to replace their chemical toilets. Some 89 toilets serving more than 200 users were installed, most with 25-liter urine tanks and some with 220-liter tanks. Ten were tested for nutrient, bacteria, and

heavy metals. Levels of thermo-tolerant coliforms were below detection level: 10 cfu/100 ml enteroccus not detectable after three months. The study found no bacterial nor parasitic infectious microorganisms (campylobacter, salmonella, cryptosporidium parvum, giardia duodenalis, or other intestinal parasites).

The urine's nutrient content was 5400 mg nitrogen (N), 360 mg phosphorus (P), and 1100 mg potassium (K).

The outdoor toilet and urinal at City Slicker Farm. The urinal drains directly to a planter growing leafy greens.

Liquid Gold in the City

Ducks and chickens cluck noisily as a visitor approaches the home of Nik Bertulis. Nik and his housemates turned a vacant lot next to their house into a tiny farm that raises all kinds of vegetables right in downtown Oakland, California. They call their farm "City Slicker Farm" and run a farmers' market on weekends. Their goal is to bring fresh fruits and vegetables and information about farming to neighborhoods in the city. (City Slicker Farm uses only urine on crops eaten by themselves, not those sold to the public.)

"Using my pee to grow food is cheap and effective, but it's also a connection to nature's cycles," he says. "The usually thoughtless daily act of urinating turns into an act of nourishing life."

To use liquid gold, Nik created a simple urinal by cutting off the top of a plastic soda bottle and attached it to a clear plastic hose with a hose clamp. It's in an enclosure outside the house with his small urine-diverting drying toilet made with a Separett diverter on a recycled 20-gallon polyethylene barrel. Urine drains via a hose that snakes into the middle of a planter made of wood pallets. The urine flows just under the root zone of chard and other greens and just above a hay bale, which slowly composts with the nitrogen addition of the urine. Once a year, Nik turns the contents of the planter, which are composted by then.

A soda bottle urinal

Nik Bertulis next to his toilet, urinal, and urine planter

Chard happily growing in urine in a planter made of discarded pallets

Photo: Tom Faber

Liquid Gold on a Small Farm

Tom Faber, a water quality specialist for the U.S. Environmental Protection Agency, collects urine to fertilize plants and speed leaf composting on his small farm in New Hampshire.

Tom relates: "I first used urine as a fertilizer when I was working on an organic farm. The farmer used compost and bloodmeal as a nitrogen source for his crops. Another intern and I grew corn in a separate 'intern garden.' The farmer was reluctant to share his expensive bloodmeal, but he said we could dilute our urine five to one with water to fertilize our corn. Sure enough, it worked. Since then I use urine, at times even at full strength, on bushes and plants, as well as on compost and woodchip piles," he says.

"Urine is a clean free fertilizer that's better used by plants than discharged to where it can create unhealthy conditions in our lakes, rivers, and estuaries."

Liquid Gold in Wales

The Centre for Alternative Technology (CAT) in Wales in the United Kingdom is an environmental center where experiments in living systems, resource recycling, and ecologically oriented building take place.

Peter Harper, Director of Biological Research at CAT, experiments with diverting and using urine for growing plants—from composting cardboard (and even books) to testing the fertilizer value on various crops. The following page shows his experiments with matching urine's nitrogen content with the carbon of cardboard and straw. Read more about his work with composting, gardening, urine diversion, composting toilets, and other ecological waste recycling systems in the book, *Lifting the Lid: An Ecological Approach to Toilet Systems*, available from CAT, Machynlleth, Powys SY20 9AZ UK, www.cat.org.uk.

Photos: Peter Harper

An experiment at the Centre for Alternative Technology shows the fertilizer effects of urine on winter onions. The three rows were planted about one foot apart, with urine applied on the far right row. The center row received some of the urine and the left row, none.

Composting with cardboard: Cardboard was cut and placed, corrugated ends up, in a container without a drain. Urine was applied intermittently. (Left) Molds appeared in two months. (Right) After a year, it is fully decomposed and ready to apply to the garden.

A strawbale urinal: An ordinary strawbale (left), with cut ends uppermost, was urinated upon intermittently. Six months to one year later (right), the center is mostly decomposed and ready to apply to soil. Peter Harper reports that this method works best with fresh urine, not stored urine.

Liquid Gold on the Roof

Conrad and Jan Geyser of Cotuit, Massachusetts use diluted urine to fertilize a sprawling vegetable and flower garden as well as leafy greens and herbs in a greenhouse on their roof. Conrad makes urine-diverting toilets to sell through Cotuit Dry Toilets.

Every few days, Conrad climbs up to his rooftop greenhouse to fertilize potted greens and herbs, such as lettuce, collards, kale, and cilantro, with diluted urine. During the summer, he applies urine to his gardens with a porous soaker hose that "sweats" water and nutrients.

Photos: Russell DeConti

(Top) Greens and herbs are fertilized with urine in a greenhouse on the roof of the home of Jan and Conrad Geyser. He collects urine from urine-diverting toilets he makes (left). During the summer months, they apply diluted urine to a large vegetable and flower garden.

Liquid Gold on the Lawn

Urine-use researcher Håkan Jonsson of the Swedish University of Agricultural Sciences uses diluted urine to fertilize and irrigate his lawn, as well as a garden and orchard. He experimented with both ejectors that dilute the urine automatically and the device he made (shown here), which distributes the urine evenly through perforated pipe while he dilutes it with a garden hose. However, he reports that applying urine without dilution also appears to work well.

Urine-fertilized gooseberries grow plentifully.

Photos: Håkan Jonsson

Håkan Jonsson fertilizes his lawn with a device he made that distributes urine evenly through perforated pipe while he dilutes it with a garden hose.

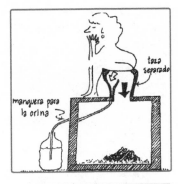

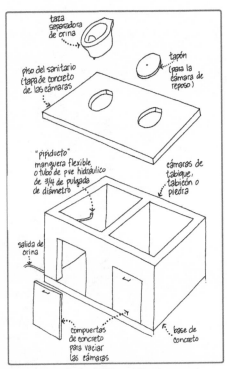

Diagrams of CITA's urine-diverting drying toilets from CITA's publications and (bottom left) from the report, Ecological Sanitation.

Urine-Diverting Toilets in Mexico

When contaminated water and water shortages affected communities in and around Mexico City, architect and political cartoonist César Añorve sought an alternative to wasteful and polluting waterflush toilets. Inspired by a system developed by social innovator Ivan Illich, he developed a waterless toilet that separates urine. He founded Centro de Innovación en Tecnología Alternativa (CITA) to create workers' cooperatives to fabricate affordable toilets of both fiberglass and cement. Today, several thousand of CITA's urine-diverting toilets are in homes in Mexico as well as in other countries, helping to reduce water use and prevent water pollution.

To add levity to the topic of excreta management so the public is more comfortable discussing it, Añorve creates publications with illustrations incorporating scatalogical images in fun and whimsical cartoons.

A poster suggests the value of urine-diverting toilets: Keeping the water clean.

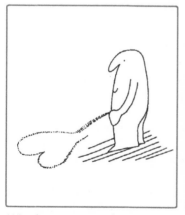

Urine love, a cartoon from Anorve's booklet, Psicoanalysis de la Zurrada

A womans' cooperative in Mexico learns how to make urine-diverting toilets.

Fertilizing Avocadoes and Nopal

In the town of Tepoztlán in Mexico, Paco and Maida Arroyo collect urine from their urine-diverting toilet, and dry urinal and pour it on their crop of nopal (edible cactus), avocados, and greens—grown both in the field and in pots.

They apply urine to the fields on rainy days, so it is automatically diluted. During dry season, they dilute it with three to five liters of water per liter of urine. Their neighbors were impressed and are now installing their own urine-diverting toilets.

The toilets and urinals were introduced to the town as a pilot program, called TepozEco, to help reduce water usage, recycle nutrients, and protect water in Tepoztlán, which is at the top of a watershed within a national park and an important biological corridor.

Photos: Sarar Transformación, Ivan Sawyer

(Top) Paco Arroyo fertilizes vegetables in planters as well as nopal cactus (left) with urine. (Above) His urine-diverting toilet and dry urinal.

Photo: David Del Porto

Outside the Ecowaters office, Carol Steinfeld picks red and gold cherry tomatoes in a well-mulched garden where she and colleagues apply their urine. Behind her, vines heavy with pole beans shade the office's south-facing windows during the summer while providing a food crop.

Liquid Gold at the Office

At the Ecowaters office in Massachusetts, we have experimented with several ways of using urine. Urine drains from a Separett urine-diverting composting toilet into a shallow oil change jug. About once a week, we empty its contents into leaf composters to add much-needed nitrogen to the plentiful carbon of the brown leaves. Ultimately, the leaves decompose into a nice compost that is mixed into the office garden. Alternately, we pour urine on surrounding trees and on a garden mulched with woodchips and watered regularly with

(Above) The urine-diverting composting toilet that drains to a small oil change jug behind it; (right) pouring the contents of the jug into a leaf composter.

rainwater. We have also combined the urine with graywater (water drained from the sink) and rainwater in an aerobic garden planter inside the office.

(Before we installed the urine-diverting toilet, a few of us fervent liquid gold users collected our urine in one-quart yogurt containers and poured it on the garden.)

Adventures in Urine Diversion

At Ecowaters' workshops and programs, urine diversion is presented as an option for composting toilets. Ecowaters, a nonprofit organization that informs the public about ecological wastewater options, installed three types of urine-diverting composting toilets at El Santuario, a small retreat lodge nestled in a serene cove on the Sea of Cortez in Baja, California Sur, Mexico. The shoreline, with its plentiful butter clams and frequent visits by dolphins and whales, is the lodge's main attraction. Its owners, Denise Jones and Bill Paff, didn't want to pollute it with wastewater. At the same time, fresh water must be trucked in from mountain springs—making it too precious to use to flush toilets.

A variety of composting toilets with urine diversion were installed using CITA fiberglass urine-diverting toilet stools. For campers, toilets made with barrels featured simple urine diverters fashioned with funnels trimmed to fit the front of the toilet openings. Urine is used to fertilize the plants around El Santuario. Visitors frequently stop by just to see the toilets and learn how they work. Many go on to make their own urine-diverting toilets for their desert homes. That's ecotourism at work.

Carol Steinfeld and a workshop participant build a portable urine-diverting composting toilet for an ecolodge in Mexico. Below, a simple urine composter is a perforated drywall bucket filled with shredded cardboard.

Right: A simple urine-diverting toilet for a surf camp in Baja California Sur, Mexico

Chris Melo traded his boat's holding tank for a urine-diverting composting toilet and a self-made urinal, Mr. PeeBuddy. He pours urine into a rain barrel that flows to drip-irrigation lines in his garden.

Liquid Gold for Boat Cuisine

Chris offers a cracker topped with homegrown basil "peesto" from his sailboat's galley.

Basil grows prolifically in Chris Melo's garden and usually makes its way into batches of pesto. His neighbors at the marina have a different name for it: Knowing it is grown with urine, they call it "peesto."

Chris, a nautical engineer who lives on his 35-foot sailboat, installed a urine-diverting composting toilet and a little urinal made of plastic bottles to replace his malodorous saltwater-flush toilet and to avoid holding tank pumpouts and overboard discharges.

Chris empties his urine tank weekly into a rain barrel that drains to drip-irrigation lines that run throughout his garden on land. During the cold months, he pours the urine down the toilet at his office. The solids tank is emptied every 40 days into a composter for further processing.

"Living this way, I'm much more aware of my ecological footprint," he says. "I'm happier knowing that I'm not harming the bay I live on."

Dr. Keith Barton looks out over his urine-fertilized backyard urban eden. Concerned about salts accumulating in his soil, he limits his salt uptake for the sake of his plants.

The Low-Salt Backyard Eden

With its profusion of greens and trees heavy with several varieties of apricots, figs, and red, purple and yellow plums, Dr. Keith Barton's half-acre backyard in Oakland, California is a counterpoint to the city that surrounds it.

Keith's sole source of fertilizer: Urine. Knowing that urine can be high in salt, he has reduced salt in his diet to avoid stressing his plants. (Salt can interfere with germination of new seeds and prevent roots from taking up water and nutrients.) Changing his diet for the sake of his plants has added another level of awareness to Keith's relationship to his food source.

A urinal drains to a graywater system that grows chicken feed and, ultimately, eggs.

Liquid Gold Grows Breakfast

It's time to feed the chickens in the backyard of the Oakland, Calif. home of Babak Tondre and Rainjita Geesler. Babak places some water hyacinth leaves in a feed bowl and the chickens eagerly peck at them, as Babak reaches into their pen to gather some eggs. Fifteen minutes later, those eggs are in a frying pan.

Babak grows the high-protein water hyacinth in his graywater system, which consists of three sequenced in-ground 50-gallon plastic bins, each filled with a different medium (gravel, wood chips, etc.) and plants (water hyacinth, reeds, and more). The home's shower and sinks drain to the system, as does a small simple waterless urinal artfully mounted on the back of a clawfoot tub, where it drains to the graywater system via the tub's overflow drain. "We grow as much food as we can in the city, just like my grandfather did, mostly because it helps us save a little money and it keeps us grounded in the garden," he says. "Working in the earth is therapy."

Liquid Gold Spray Feeds the Trees

Applying urine to leaves, not roots, is its most effective use, according to Paul William. "Foliar feeding is much more efficient at stimulating plant growth than fertilizing via the root system only," he says. "The leaves respond within hours of the application."

Paul William applies diluted urine to fruit trees.

Certainly his yard in California's suburban Silicon Valley attests: He grows many varieties of plums, peaches, nectarines, apricots, apples, pears, pawpaws, cherimoyas, avocados, passion fruit, prickly pear cactus, citrus, persimmons, grapes, olives, pineapple, pineapple guava, and figs.

To determine the best dilution to prevent the mix from getting too salty, he uses a TDS (total dissolved solids) meter available from hydroponic garden supply stores. "My tap water has 600 ppm (parts per million) as a result of the chlorine salts before I add any urine. I add urine until I get around 1,700 ppm." He also adds a bit of soap so the spray better penetrates the leaves.

Rose William holds a yellow strawberry guava from a tree fertilized with urine foliar spray.

"Urine foliar feeding is amazing," he says. "My friends are having huge success growing all kinds of tropical plants doing it, and my temperate plants are so lush and green, it boggles the mind!"

Flushing Green in a Nitrogen-Sensitive Zone

When Seth Wilkinson and Alison Flynn were designing a house that would have lower environmental impact, they at first considered installing a composting toilet. The pair live on Cape Cod, a region

grappling with nitrogen pollution affecting lakes, seashores, and groundwater. Ultimately, they sought something more appealing to the mainstream yet affordable and effective for managing nitrogen.

They installed a Wost-Man Ekologen DS urine-diverting flush toilet. Inside, a small drained basin is partitioned in the front of the toilet bowl, so urine is caught and flushed with a tablespoon of water. Solids are flushed away via a 1.2-gallon flush to a conventional septic system.

Alison Flynn next to her urine-diverting flush toilet that flushes urine to a 1,000-gallon tank.

The urine-water mixture drains to a 1,000-gallon in-ground tank. When it fills up (about once a year) a float switch turns on an alert light. The urine then either drains via an overflow pipe to the septic system or Flynn hoses it onto piles of composting leaves and well-mulched gardens. It has no significant odor, she reports.

However, to make their system more of a demonstration for homeowners who would not use the urine-water as she does, Alison and Seth are installing an engineered GROW™ (Garden Recycling Of Wastewater) system that will feature plants specially chosen for their nitrogen- and salt-uptake abilities but blend in with their landscaping. It's a true growaway strategy for sequestering nitrogen and carbon, a theme in keeping with their "petroleum-free" ecologically oriented house.

Landscape planner Anja Brüll applies urine around the well-mulched drip line of a tree (where rain falls from the tree's branches) outside Ecowaters' office.

Many find that once they start using liquid gold, flushing it away feels wasteful. Pouring one's urine on the soil to nourish a garden is a direct and daily connection to the land that supports and feeds us. It's a nurturing act versus the more mechanical act of flushing our urine to a wastewater treatment plant miles away for disposal.

It's a simple and empowering act that allows us to step into our place in the nutrient cycle—a way to reconnect consciously and productively with the web of life and energy of which we are a part.

You might consider it a spiritual practice.

John Cossham, known professionally as juggler-unicyclist Professor Fiddlesticks, pours his household's urine into his compost pile behind his home in the city of York in England. He also applies urine directly to areas near his garden. "You should see the squashes I get!" he says.

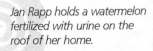

Jan Rapp holds a watermelon fertilized with urine on the roof of her home.

Conrad Geyser stands next to his urine tanks to which his urine-diverting toilets drain. These drain downhill to soaker hoses in his garden.

Sven Ingvar-Nilsson's toilet in Sweden. The coffin-like base contains the solids container, which he takes outside to burn the contents.

Frequently Asked Questions

Why does urine contain nutrients?

We consume a lot of animal and vegetable protein, and that's where nitrogen comes from. But our bodies can only use a certain amount of that protein to build cells. What's left over is digested and turned into other compounds, which in addition to broken-down cells and metabolic waste products, make up the nitrogen content of our urine. This is in the forms of urea, creatine, ammonia and some uric acid.

Why is urine yellow?

Urine is the filtration byproduct of the kidneys. The kidneys keep the salt content of the blood constant and filter waste out of the bloodstream. So the main components of urine are salt, water, and waste products. The major waste product from cells in the body is ammonia, and the major waste product from blood is a broken form of heme called bilirubin. In the liver, each of these is converted into a less hazardous form: Ammonia is converted to urea, and bilirubin is degraded to urobilins. Urobilins, which come from degraded pigments, are yellow. The more watered down the urine (if you drink a lot), the lighter the urine.

Urine appears to kill grass. Are you sure it's OK to use it on plants?

Urine's sodium chloride (table salt), uric acid, and concentrated urea can kill grass if it is applied to the same place continually. Mainly, the problem occurs with dogs and cats that urinate in the same spot every day. The soil organisms responsible for converting these constituents into plant food have insufficient time to do their work before the next deposit hits the spot. Irrigating with fresh water will solve the problem, because it dilutes the concentrate so it can drain into the soil.

Won't it smell?

It might. The key is not to let it decompose into ammonia, which smells really bad. The soil contains an enzyme called "urase" that catalyzes the urea in urine to form ammonia. Further, urine decomposes into sulfur-containing compounds, which give stale urine an odor. However, if you dilute urine or pour it on healthy soil with lots of life, air pockets, and carbon, beneficial bacteria convert it to a form that plants can use and the urine will have less chance to produce odors.

I hear that urine is salty. Will that hurt my plants?

Because most of us in the western world consume way too much salt, all but a small fraction needed to sustain cell life is excreted in our urine. In a garden with poor drainage, the salt will accumulate and stress some plants. Make sure that urine is applied to areas where rain or other water flushes it periodically. If salt is a major concern, such as where the tap water is also salty, remove the salt with halophytes. Halophytes are plants that take up salt and deposit it in special glands in their leaves; in this way, they mine and remove the salt from soils. Some plants of this type are atriplex (salt bush), tamarix (salt cedar), and spartina (salt water cord grass).

Won't I get sick if I use urine on food crops?

Urine is typically sterile before it leaves the body in healthy populations; therefore, the risk is extremely low. However, some disease-causing organisms can appear in urine—usually in tropical settings. The big disease risk is in untreated feces that contain bacteria, viruses, and parasites from a diseased person. The good news is that the organisms in the soil destroy these germs in a few hours, particularly in a warm climate.

How much fertilizer value is in a gallon of straight urine?

The amount of nitrogen varies widely, depending on how much protein was ingested. The average adult in the U.S. produces about 11 grams (.024 pounds) of nitrogen daily. That count is lower in populations with lower protein diets. Urine's NPK value is about 11-1-2.5, although this varies among populations.

Is urine fertilizer especially good for particular crops?

Urine is higher in nitrogen than it is in potassium and phosphorus (the other main mineral ingredients in fertilizers). Nitrogen is especially needed for plant leaf growth, so leafy greens and grasses benefit greatly. Corn needs lots of nitrogen. Phosphorus is valuable for root growth, and potassium helps with the flowering and fruiting process. Plants need all these minerals to thrive, in addition to a healthy soil with lots of carbon (to give it structure) and beneficial bacterial life to convert minerals to a form that plants can consume and to fight off disease.

References

Urine Lore:

Paul Spinrad, *The RE/Search Guide to Bodily Fluids* (Juno Books, 1999; ISBN: 1890451045)

John G. Bourke, *Scatologic Rites of All Nations* (W. H. Lowdermilk, 1891; reprinted by Kessinger Publishing Company, 2003; ISBN 0766161927)

Egyptian pregnancy and baby gender test: Moustafa Gadalia, *Historical Deception: The Untold Story of Ancient Egypt* (Tehuti Research Foundation, 1999)

Mongolian horse warriors: Daniel J. Boorstin, *The Discoverers* (Random House)

Pesticide and herbicide in Senegal: "Benign Urine," *New Internationalist,* June 1998, issue 302

Selling urine in 19th century Britain: BBC4, "Taking the P*** Out of London"

Fading freckles: A. Monroe Aurand, Jr., *Popular Home Remedies and Superstitions of the Pennsylvania Germans* (Aurand Press)

Snake bite cure: Charles W. Eastman, Jr., and Anne M. Eastman, "Perspectives '76," Regional Center for Educational Training for the New Hampshire-Vermont Bicentennial Educational Resources Program)

Diagnosis with urine: Patsy Evans, Senior Lecturer, Department of Pathology and Lab Medicine and V. Robinson, *The Story of Medicine* (The New Home Library, 1943)

Urine use by baseball players. Slate magazine, www.slate.com, May 17, 2004

Pee Outside Day: *The Ecologist,* July 2000

"Urine is the key!": Dan Brown, *Deception Point* (Pocket Books, 2002)

Urine Therapy:

Flora Peschek-Bohmer and Gisela Schreiber, *Urine Therapy: Nature's Elixir for Good Health* (Healing Arts Press, 1999)

Michael Braunstein, "Urine Therapy," Heartland Healing Arts Center Web site (Omaha, Nebraska)

J. Eldor, "Urotherapy for Patients with Cancer," *Med Hypotheses,* 1997; 48:309-315

American Cancer Society's Guide to Complementary and Alternative Methods, American Cancer Society, 2000

Swami Satyananda Saraswati, *Amaroli* (Bihar School of Yoga, 1991)

Science and Technology:

David Del Porto and Carol Steinfeld, *The Composting Toilet System Book* (Ecowaters Books, Concord, Massachusetts 2000)

Caroline Höglund, *Evaluation of Microbial Health Risks Associated with the Reuse of Source-separated Human Urine* (Royal Institute of Technology Library, Sweden, 2001)

Håkan Jonsson, Björn Vinneras, Caroline Höglund, Thor-Axel Stenström, "Source Separation of Urine" (Wasser & Boden, 51/11, 21-25 ISSN 0043-0951, Berlin, Germany 1999)

Thor-Axel Stenström, Caroline Höglund, Håkan Jonsson, "Evaluation of microbial risks and faecal contamination of urine diverting sewage systems" (Wasser & Boden. 51/10, 11-14 ISSN 0043-0951, Berlin, Germany 1999)

Caroline Höglund and Thor-Axel Stenström, "Survival of Cryptosporidium parvum in source separated human urine" (*Canadian Journal of Microbiology* 45: 1-7 1999)

K. Sundberg, "What Does Household Wastewater Contain?" Report 4425 (Swedish Environmental Protection Agency, Stockholm, Sweden 1995)

Håkan Jonsson, "Assessment of Sanitation Systems and Reuse of Urine," *Swedish University of Agricultural Sciences Proceedings of the SIDA Ecological Alternatives in Sanitation Conference,* August, 1997

Uno Winblad, ed., *Ecological Sanitation* (Sida, Stockholm, Sweden 1997)

Soils for the Management of Organic Wastes and Wastewaters (Madison, Wisconsin: Soil Science Society of America, 1977)

ASHRAE Handbook & Product Directory, 1977 Fundamentals, Psychrometric Tables (American Society of Heating, Refrigerating and Air Conditioning Engineers, New York, NY)

Mats Wolgast, "Rena vatten—om tankar i kretslopp" (Creanom HB, Uppsala, Sweden 1993)

Jan-Olof Drangert, "Perceptions, Urine Blindness and Urban Agriculture," *Ecological Alternatives in Sanitation, Proceedings from Sida Sanitation Workshop,* August, 1997

Ralf Otterpohl, University of Hamburg, personal correspondence, 1998

Caroline Schönning, *Recommendations for the reuse of urine and faeces in order to minimise the risk for disease transmission,* Swedish Institute for Infectious Disease Control, 2003

Green to Gold:

Urine Separation—Closing the Nutrient Cycle, (Stockholm Water Company et al, Stockholm, Sweden 2002)

Lifting the Lid: An Ecological Approach to Toilet Systems (Centre for Alternative Technology, Machynlleth, Powys, Wales, 1998)

Anna Edey, *Solviva* (Trailblazer Press, Martha's Vineyard, Massachusetts 1997)

César Añorve et al, *Psicoanalysis de la Zurrada* (Cuernavaca, Mexico, 1999)